Treasure Island

Robert Louis Stevenson

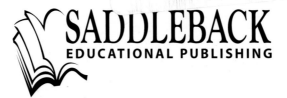

SADDLEBACK
EDUCATIONAL PUBLISHING

D1167237

Saddleback's *Illustrated Classics*™

SADDLEBACK
EDUCATIONAL PUBLISHING
www.sdlback.com

ISBN-13: 978-1-56254-948-0
ISBN-10: 1-56254-948-0
eBook: 978-1-60291-173-4

Printed in Guangzhou, China
NOR/0213/CA21300171

17 16 15 14 13   1 2 3 4 5

Welcome to
Saddleback's *Illustrated Classics*™

We are proud to welcome you to Saddleback's *Illustrated Classics*™. Saddleback's *Illustrated Classics*™ was designed specifically for the classroom to introduce readers to many of the great classics in literature. Each text, written and adapted by teachers and researchers, has been edited using the Dale-Chall vocabulary system. In addition, much time and effort has been spent to ensure that these high-interest stories retain all of the excitement, intrigue, and adventure of the original books.

With these graphically *Illustrated Classics*™, you learn what happens in the story in a number of different ways. One way is by reading the words a character says. Another way is by looking at the drawings of the character. The artist can tell you what kind of person a character is and what he or she is thinking or feeling.

This series will help you to develop confidence and a sense of accomplishment as you finish each novel. The stories in Saddleback's *Illustrated Classics*™ are fun to read. And remember, fun motivates!

Overview

Everyone deserves to read the best literature our language has to offer. Saddleback's *Illustrated Classics*™ was designed to acquaint readers with the most famous stories from the world's greatest authors, while teaching essential skills. You will learn how to:

- Establish a purpose for reading
- Activate prior knowledge
- Evaluate your reading
- Listen to the language as it is written
- Extend literary and language appreciation through discussion and writing activities.

Reading is one of the most important skills you will ever learn. It provides the key to all kinds of information. By reading the *Illustrated Classics*™, you will develop confidence and the self-satisfaction that comes from accomplishment—a solid foundation for any reader.

Step-By-Step

The following is a simple guide to using and enjoying each of your *Illustrated Classics*™. To maximize your use of the learning activities provided, we suggest that you follow these steps:

1. *Listen!* We suggest that you listen to the read-along. (At this time, please ignore the beeps.) You will enjoy this wonderfully dramatized presentation.

2. *Post-reading Activities.* You have successfully read the story and listened to the audio presentation. Now answer the multiple-choice questions and other activities in the Study Guide.

Remember,

"Today's readers are tomorrow's leaders."

Robert Louis Stevenson

Robert Louis Balfour Stevenson, who came to be known as Louis to avoid confusion with an older cousin, was born in Edinburgh, Scotland, in 1850. An industrious person, he carried two books with him always—one to read and one in which to write.

His imagination for a story was sparked often by simple clues. For example, Stevenson's first successful book, *Treasure Island*, written in 1881, was reputedly inspired by a treasure map and a twelve-year-old boy. Many of the adventures are similar to ones Stevenson experienced as a child.

Stevenson, a collector of ideas, often borrowed from other writers, but his own style was unmistakable. In 1885, while hard at work on *Kidnapped, A Child's Garden of Verses* was published. In 1886, *The Strange Case of Dr. Jekyll and Mr. Hyde* was first published. In 1887, he began *The Master of the Ballantrae*, finishing it in 1889. Stevenson died in 1894, never completing his final book, *Weir of Hermiston*, referred to by many as his finest work.

Although plagued by illness throughout his life, Stevenson was a restless adventurer. He traveled extensively, married an American, and retreated for health reasons to the South Sea Islands in 1889. Here, he established himself as the "tusitala," or the "teller of tales," to the natives.

Robert Louis Stevenson

Treasure Island

Squire Trelawney

Long John Silver

Jim Hawkins

Billy Bones

Dr. Livesey

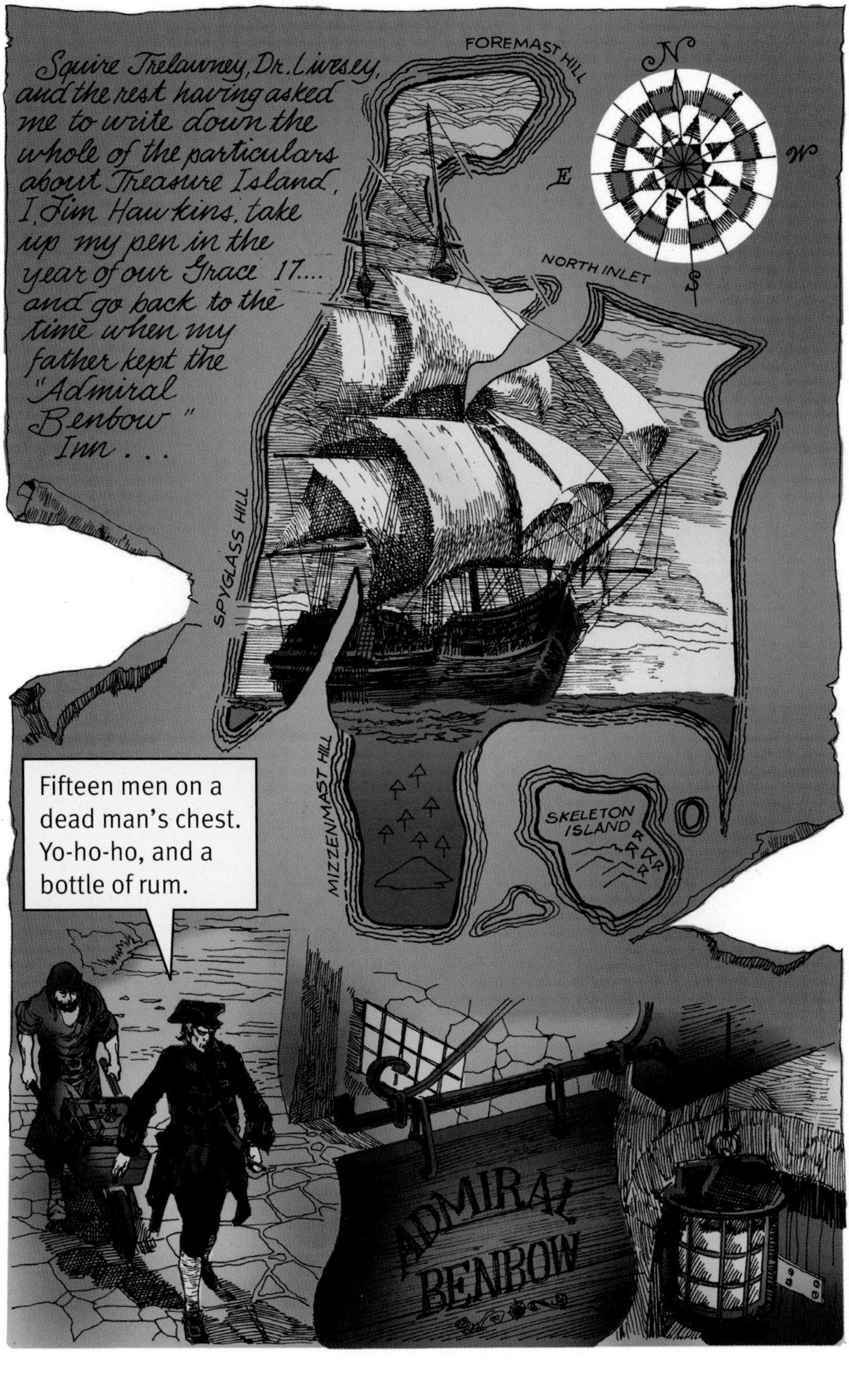
Squire Trelawney, Dr. Livesey, and the rest having asked me to write down the whole of the particulars about Treasure Island, I, Jim Hawkins, take up my pen in the year of our Grace 17... and go back to the time when my father kept the "Admiral Benbow" Inn . . .
FOREMAST HILL
N
E
W
S
NORTH INLET
SPYGLASS HILL
MIZZENMAST HILL
SKELETON ISLAND
Fifteen men on a dead man's chest. Yo-ho-ho, and a bottle of rum.
ADMIRAL BENBOW

I'll never forget the day Billy Bones came into my life. He arrived at my father's inn and asked for a glass of rum.

This is a pleasant spot with a nice view of the sea, sir. Do you get many people coming to stay?

No, sir. I'm sorry to say. It's very quiet here.

And so he came to stay.

Bring in my chest. I'll stay awhile and trouble you little for I'm a plain man. I just like to look at the sea.

Here is some gold. Just let me know when I owe you more.

He was a quiet man, and we could see he did not want to run in to other sailors. One day he pulled me aside and said...

You, Jim, keep watch for a sailor with one leg. Do your job well and I'll pay you for it.

Yes, sir.

He stayed month after month but only talked to people when he was drunk. One night when Dr. Livesey had come to see my father, who was ill. Bones started...

Quiet over there!

You keep on drinking that rum and you'll end up killing yourself.

Bones got mad and came at the Doctor with a knife.

A few days later Bones was surprised by an unexpected guest...

Put that knife away this minute or I'll have you hanged.

For a minute we thought there'd be trouble, but Bones gave in.

Ah Bill, I haven't seen you in years.

So you finally found me, Black Dog. Well...what do you want?

I want a glass of rum. Then we'll sit and talk like old shipmates.

They talked quietly for awhile. All of a sudden they began to shout and Black Dog took off running.

The captain staggered inside and fell on the floor. Just then Dr. Livesey stopped to see my father.

What shall we do?

I warned him. He's had a heart attack just as I said he would. Get me a pan.

I'll bleed him just enough to keep him quiet.

When I stopped in to see him later, he was weak but worried.

Jim, it's my sea chest they'll want if they kill me. You tell the doctor to get everyone up here when they come.

They can take care of Flint's crew. I was Old Flint's first mate and the only one who knows his secret. But don't you tell anyone what I've said unless they put the Black Spot on me or you see a sailor with one leg. You hear, Jim?

That night my father died and I didn't think of anything else until the next morning.

I'm blind. Will anybody tell me where I am.

At the Admiral Benbow Inn, sir.

He asked to be taken inside but when I held out my arm...

Take me right to Captain Bones or I'll break your arm.

He gave a note to Bones and then left quickly.

Six hours to go. I'll make it yet.

But as Bones stood up, he grabbed his throat and fell to the floor—dead!

Mother!

I told my mother all I knew and we tried to get some help. No one would do anything except ride to find the doctor.

We went through Bones' sea chest and my mother took what money he owed her.

If no one will help us then we'll go back alone. Come, Jim.

I am an honest woman. I'll take only what is mine.

Suddenly we heard a strange whistle coming from the hill outside.

Come, Jim, I have what I need.

I'll take this too, just to be sure.

The pirates went right to the inn and were ordered to go in and search.

A moment later the strange whistle sounded again. I had thought that it was the pirates' signal to attack, but it seemed to fill them with fear.

Pew, someone beat us to it. They've gone through the sea chest.

It's that boy! I wish I'd put out his eyes. Go, men, and find him.

There's Dirk again. We have to go, men.

You're so close to getting thousands of dollars and you're going to leave?

Don't stand there talking, Pew. Let's go!

His friends left without him, and Pew ran on...to his death.

After a useless chase, the riders, who were government men sent by the doctor, came back to the inn.

You're right, son. Dogger, put the boy on the horse with you and we'll go report to Dr. Livesey.

What were they after?

I think I have it in my pocket. I'd like to put it in a safe place.

Dr. Livesey was having dinner with Squire Trelawney.

Come in, Mr. Danse.

Good evening, friend Jim. What bring you here?

Officer Danse told them what had happened, and the two men were very surprised and interested.

Mr. Danse, you're a good man.

I'll keep Hawkins here and give him some dinner.

While I ate a big dinner Mr. Danse and the men talked. Finally Danse left.

And now, Livesey...

You've heard of this Flint, haven't you?

The evil Flint was well-known to the Squire as was the fact that he had buried treasure.

If there is a clue to his treasure here, I'll rent a ship. We'll find the treasure if it takes a year.

We'll open these papers if Jim says we can.

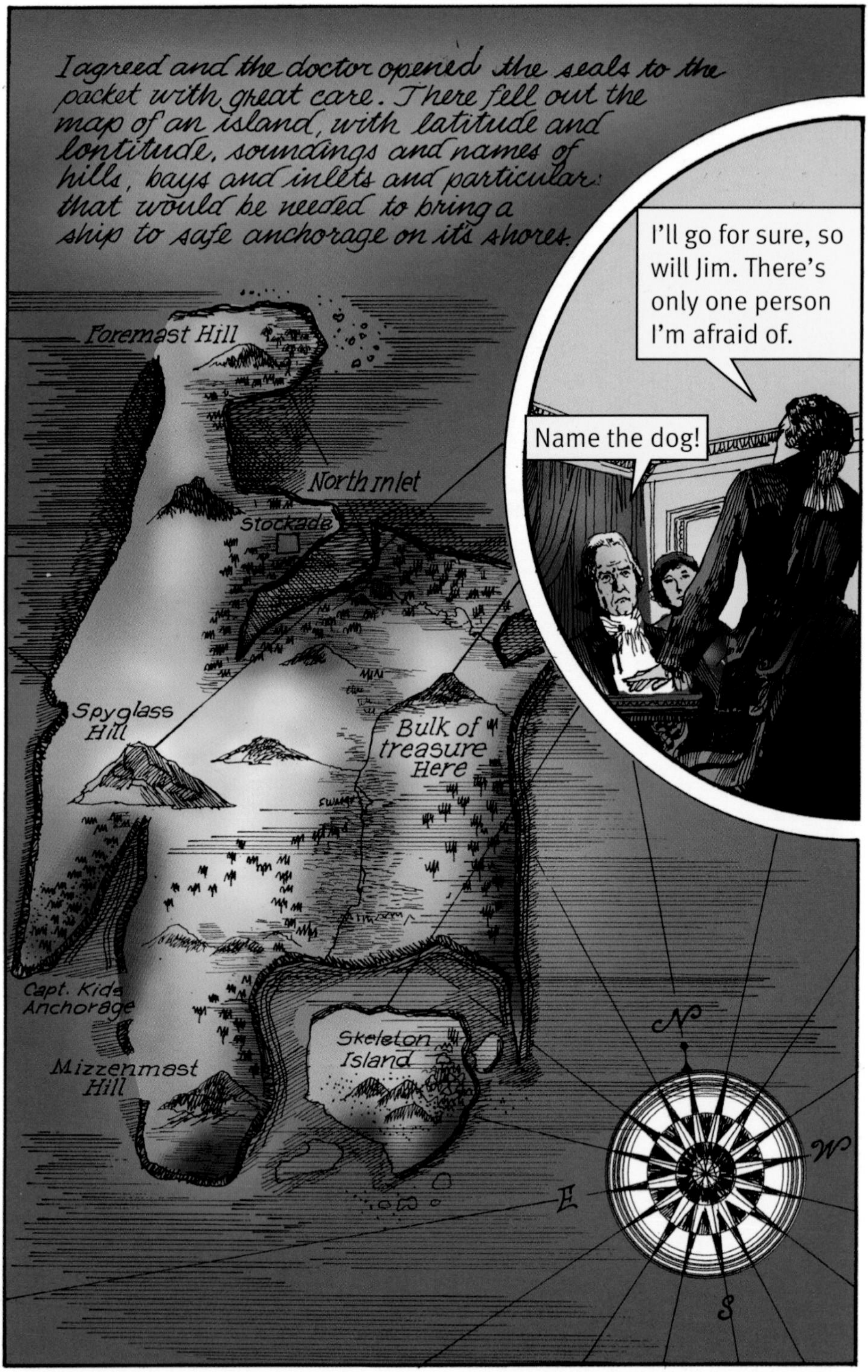
I agreed and the doctor opened the seals to the packet with great care. There fell out the map of an island, with latitude and lontitude, soundings and names of hills, bays and inlets and particulars that would be needed to bring a ship to safe anchorage on it's shores.
I'll go for sure, so will Jim. There's only one person I'm afraid of.
Name the dog!
Foremast Hill
North Inlet
Stockade
Spyglass Hill
Bulk of treasure Here
Capt. Kidd Anchorage
Mizzenmast Hill
Skeleton Island
N
W
E
S

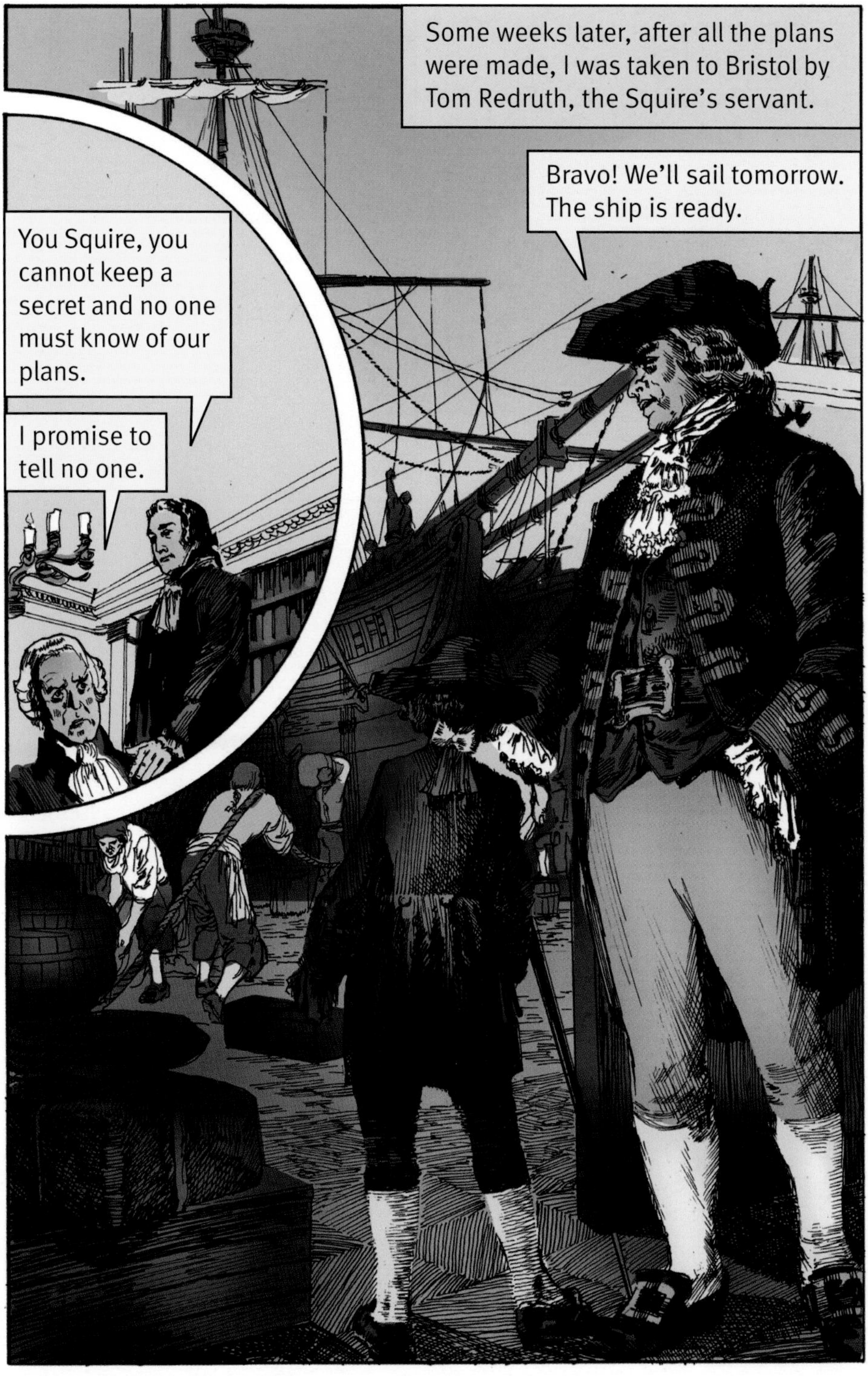
Some weeks later, after all the plans were made, I was taken to Bristol by Tom Redruth, the Squire's servant.
You Squire, you cannot keep a secret and no one must know of our plans.
I promise to tell no one.
Bravo! We'll sail tomorrow. The ship is ready.

Squire gave me a note to take to John Silver, owner of the Spyglass tavern, who had the job of a cook on our ship.

The Squire had told me that John had only one leg, and I was afraid he might be the sailor Bones had told me to watch for. But he seemed so nice that I soon forgot my fear.

All of a sudden a sailor saw me and ran.

Stop him! That's Black Dog!

Run and get him, Harry. He didn't pay his bill. Black what?

I was again afraid but Silver was too smart for me. Harry came back without Black Dog and Silver yelled at him terribly. So I was again sure Silver was not a man for me to fear.

I'll go with you to the Captain. This is important business, and he must know about it.

That afternoon we all went aboard the Hispaniola, our ship, to give her a final check.

Captain Smollett is here, sir. He wants to speak with you.

Show him in.

I don't like this trip. I don't like the men and I don't like my officer. That's what I've come to tell you.

Maybe you don't like the men who hired you either.

Stay awhile. You have said too much and too little, Captain. You don't like this trip. Tell me why?

I hear you have a map of an island where treasure is buried. This island is located...

I never told a soul.

Everyone on this ship knows about it, sir. This trip could end in the death of every one of us!

He gave the exact location.

Do you fear a mutiny?

To protect this ship we must make new plans. You must do what I ask or I shall quit.

The Squire was angry about the changes but they were made. Just before sunrise the next day we set sail.

Ours was a fine ship with a good crew and a captain who knew his business. Our trip to Treasure Island was a good one.

Long John was obeyed by everyone in the crew. He always seemed glad to see me when I came into his galley, which was very neat.

The captain said he must have been wrong about the crew for they worked very hard...and he learned to love the ship.

Come in, Jim, and I'll tell you a story or two. This is my parrot, Captain Flint, who was just telling me we're in for a good trip.

Pieces of eight. Pieces of eight.

She's sailing well, sir, but we're not there yet.

The Squire tried to keep the men happy. He kept a barrel of apples on the deck and let the men help themselves whenever they wanted, and he gave them extra rum.

You're spoiling the men. They will get lazy.

But good did come of the apple barrel. One night I climbed in to find an apple and almost fell asleep there when a heavy man came up and sat down against it.

Silver told of how he was an officer on Flint's ship and of how he lost his leg and Pew lost his eyes.

It wasn't long before I knew that our lives would depend on what I heard.

Flint was a good pirate. The best!

Yes, I've seen Flint's ship covered with blood and ready to sink because of all the gold she was carrying.

Most of the men on board were Flint's and they were glad to be here. Flint was afraid of me and the men know it. They trust me, mate, and you can, too.

I didn't like this job until I had this little talk with you. But I like it now. Let's shake hands on it.

Then Silver gave a low whistle and a third man joined them.

How long are we going to wait? I want to get at their wine.

As long as I can. The Captain is sailing the ship for us. The Doctor and the Squire will find the treasure and help us get it on board. I say we'll wait until I think the time is right! Get me an apple, Dirk.

You can guess how afraid I was....

Forget that. Let's go get some rum.

Dirk, thank God, went to get a cup instead.

None of the other Doctor's men want to join us.

Just then I heard a cry....

Land Ho!

Everyone rushed to the deck, and I climbed out of the barrel.

Doctor, get the Captain and Squire to the cabin. I must tell you all some news.

When they were all there, I told them what I had heard.

That Silver is something.

Captain, you were right. I will follow your orders.

I think we should plan carefully and try to take them by surprise.

You can count on my men and myself.

That is three plus ourselves. I wonder if any of the crew will help us. We'll have to find out as soon as we can.

And so it looked like our six grown men against nineteen of them.

We anchored the next morning and knew the mutiny might happen any minute.

If I give another order I think the crew will attack. We had better let one man handle them.

Who is that?

Silver, sir. He wants to keep things quiet, too. Let the men go ashore and Silver will bring them back quiet as lambs.

It's a hot day men. If anyone wants to go ashore he may do so for the afternoon.

After saying this the Captain left and Silver took charge. It was plain to the crew that Silver was their captain now.

For some crazy reason I decided to go ashore with the men so I hid in one of the smaller boats.

Jim, is that you? Keep your head down.

Jim! Jim!

I ran until I thought I would drop.

I enjoyed exploring the island until I heard two people talking close by.

I tried to get closer so I could hear.

At last I could see as well.

I'm giving you a chance to join us. Now make up your mind.

I'd rather lose a hand than join you.

I'd found an honest man who would join our side but a horrible scream made me forget for a minute.

In God's name what was that?

I guess that was poor Allen.

At this Tom jumped forward.

God rest his soul. Kill me too if you can catch me.

And Tom took off for the beach but he did not get very far.

Silver was on top of him in a moment and stabbed him twice with his knife. For the next few minutes my head felt like it was going around in circles.

When my head cleared I ran faster that I had ever run before, until...

What's that? A monkey or a bear?

Whatever it was ran off like a deer making a wide circle...

Not knowing what the thing was, I thought I would have been better off staying with Long John.

Who are you?

Ben Gunn and I haven't spoken to a human in three years.

Many a night I've dreamed of cheese.

If I ever get back to my ship you shall have some.

But how am I to get back to my ship?

Not you, I know.

I told him the whole story....

You just trust old Ben Gunn.

He told me how he'd been on Flint's ship, The Walrus, when Flint came to the island and buried the treasure and how when on another ship he'd begged the captain to stop and search for it. But when after twelve days the hadn't found it, they left Ben with just a gun and a shovel and sailed off. He had lived on berries, goat's meat, and fish and had found the treasure which he would share with those who safely took him home.

But how am I to get back to my ship?

Well, I have a little boat just under that white rock....

Just then we heard the sound of a cannon.

They've started to fight. Follow me!

We ran toward the ship until suddenly...

It seems that just after I left the ship, the Doctor and Mr. Hunter came ashore, too, to have a look at Flint's old fort. Some happenings I knew nothing about led to what we now saw. Let me go back then and tell you about it.

The Doctor left Hunter to guard the small boat and had gone on alone.

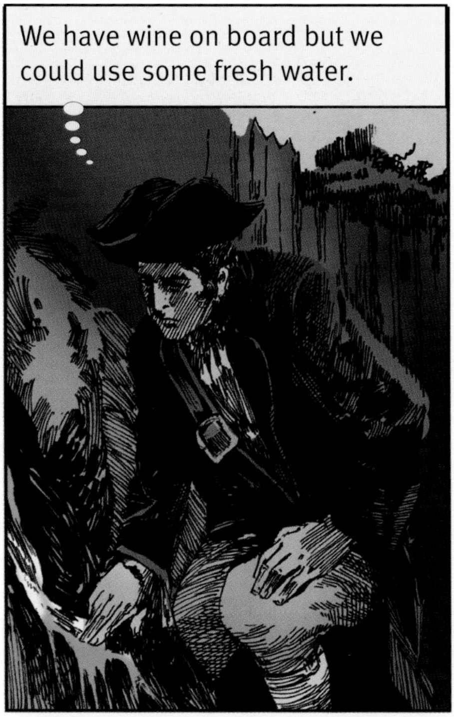
We have wine on board but we could use some fresh water.

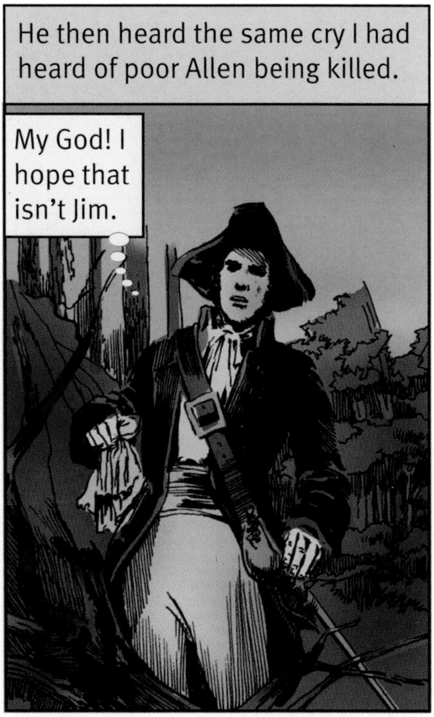
He then heard the same cry I had heard of poor Allen being killed.
My God! I hope that isn't Jim.

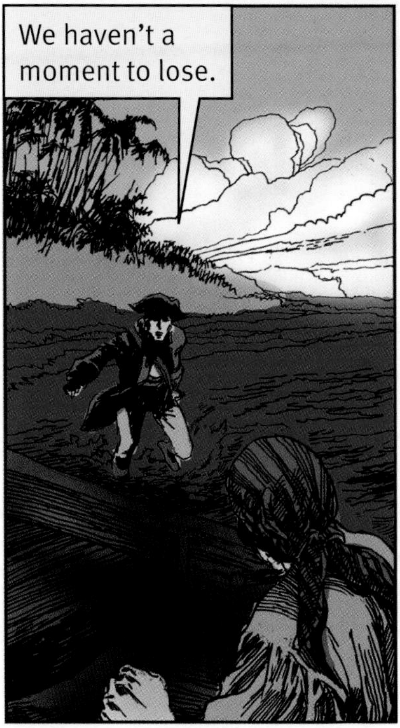
We haven't a moment to lose.

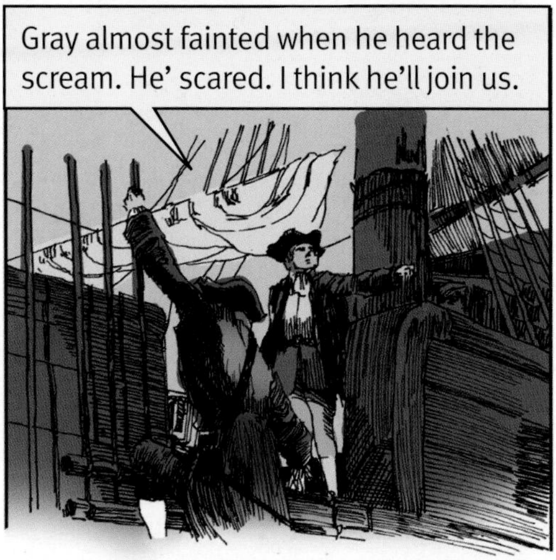
Gray almost fainted when he heard the scream. He' scared. I think he'll join us.

We decided to fight from the fort. The Doctor with Hunter and Joyce took food and guns to the fort while the Captain and Squire stayed on board to guard the ship.

Leaving Hunter and Joyce to guard the fort, the Doctor returned to the others on the boat.

Gray, I order you to follow your captain.

Gray joined them, and the boat headed for shore.

Suddenly they saw that the cannon on deck was being loaded.

Israel Hands was Flint's best gunner.

Mr. Trelawney, shoot Mr. Hands if you are able.

But just as Squire fired, Hands ducked, and another man fell.

They'll have to run fast!

They're only taking one boat. The rest are coming by shore to cut us off.

They were just a few feet from shore when a cannonball fell near them and flooded the boat.

Watch it men. The boat is sinking.

They waded to shore as fast as they could and headed for the fort. Just as they got over the wall seven mutineers showed up.

Good work men. It looks like one of them is dead.

One man was dead, and the others ran. But a few seconds later a gun sounded from the bushes.

They got Tom.

Tom was dying and asked for a prayer...

Please, sir, a prayer.

...without another word, he died.

Back to my story, then...I asked Ben Gunn to come to the fort, but he wanted to be sure the Squire would share the treasure with him.

And when they want to see Ben Gunn, you can find him where you found him today.

The pirates began firing from the ship and so it was several hours before I made my return. They were all glad to see me.

I told my story and found out from the Doctor that Ben's strangeness was not unusual.

I think he might be crazy.

No, I think he's all right.

He wanted cheese did he?

Yes, sir, cheese!

I happen to carry cheese in my tobacco box. You take it to Ben Gunn.

Before supper we buried old Tom.

After we ate, we talked about our plans.

There were nineteen of them, but two are gone.

We'll keep after them until we've won or they run away with the Hispaniola.

It will be the first ship I've ever lost.

With luck, too much rum or malaria will take care of them within the week.

I slept very well that night but woke up early.

They've put up a flag of truce.

It's Captain Silver. I've come to talk.

Watch out, men! This could be a trick.

Captain Silver... who is he?

Me, sir. The men made me Captain after you left. Let me come and talk to you.

You'd better sit down.

It's a cold day to sit on the sand.

As my cook I treated you well, as a mutineer you will hang!

Well now, we'll give you a choice. Give us the map and let us get the treasure. Once we have it safely on board we will let you come too. We'll drop you somewhere with the food and tell the first ship we see to come after you.

Now listen to me. You send your men up here one by one without their guns and I'll take you all to England for a fair trial. These are my last words about it. Either you do as I say or I'll shoot you the next time we meet.

Help me up.

Not I!

Laugh at me, will you. Before the hour's gone I'll give you something to laugh at. Those that die will be the lucky ones!

I gave Silver my finals words on the subject. Soon we should know what will happen.

The Captain told us his plan and after getting things ready, we waited.

Suddenly the fighting began.

All hands to the battle.

In the first few minutes two were killed, one ran, but four came right at us.

Hunter...watch out!

Fight them out in the open men. Use your swords.

Go around the house, men, around the house.

Poor Hunter was knocked out with his own gun.

In a few seconds all that was left of the pirates were the five who had died.

We saw right away what the battle had cost us.

But five of them are dead.

We have better odds than we started with.

Later that afternoon the Doctor went to find Ben Gunn, and I took off to find Ben's boat.

It was dark by the time I found it so I planned to paddle out to the Hispaniola, cut her ropes and let her float where she may.

I did this easily but got carried along with the current.

I'm drifting toward the open sea.

I began to pray thinking I was lost for good. I fell asleep and dreamed.

To my surprise I woke up still alive— not in the open sea, but somewhere on the other side of the island.

I just floated along for a while until I saw the Hispaniola with nobody on deck steering her.

Those pirates must have left or be as drunk as can be.

I thought I might be able to sail her back to the Captain.

I got aboard but a wave sank my little boat and I had no way to escape.

I found one pirate dead and Israel Hands drunk and hurt.

Brandy, get me some brandy.

Are you all right, Mr. Hands?

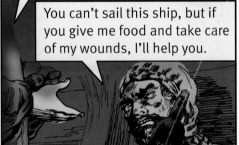

Looking around I found a bottle for Hands and some food for me.

I'd better hurry.

I am your Captain until you're told otherwise, Mr. Hands.

You can't sail this ship, but if you give me food and take care of my wounds, I'll help you.

I told him I would do as he asked, and in a few minutes we were headed for the North Inlet. I was pleased and proud but frightened, too.

Get me a bottle of wine, Jim. This brandy is too strong.

I couldn't believe anything was too strong for him, so...

I watched to see what he would do.

He took a knife from his dead mate and I knew I had to be more careful.

Maybe I'll make it without trouble.

It was difficult sailing but with Hands' help it went smoothly until...

I jumped aside and the wheel spun out of control.

No you don't, Mr. Hands.

Stay where you are.

But my guns were wet and needed to be reloaded.

Suddenly the ship hit ground.

I climbed the ropes and reloaded my guns.

Stay where you are, Hands, or I'll shoot to kill.

His knife sailed up and pinned me to the mast just as both guns went off.

Hands fell into the sea, and after freeing myself I cut the sails to keep her pretty still and started ashore.

Now to get back to the fort.

At last I came to the clearing.

There doesn't seem to be anyone here.

I knew something was wrong when I heard...

Pieces of eight! Pieces of eight!

At the sound of Silver's parrot I turned and ran into a pair of arms that closed about me and held me.

Who's there? Bring a torch, Dirk.

So it's Jim Hawkins. I find that interesting.

I want to know where my friends are and what's been going on.

Yesterday the Doctor came and told me the ship was gone. Said my men sold out—gave me some food and left. Don't know where they are.

I have something to tell you too.

I was excited and told how I had heard their plans while hiding in the apple barrel and then how I cut the ship loose so they'd never find her.

Let me live and I'll save you from hanging. Kill me and you'll be in even more trouble.

I'm Captain here! You'll do as I say.

Kill you I will.

I've had enough listening to you, Silver.

You who wants to see who's captain, take out your sword. I'll see the color of your blood.

No one moved, but my heart pounded so I thought I would explode.

I must have
looked so
surprised
that he asked
me no more
questions.

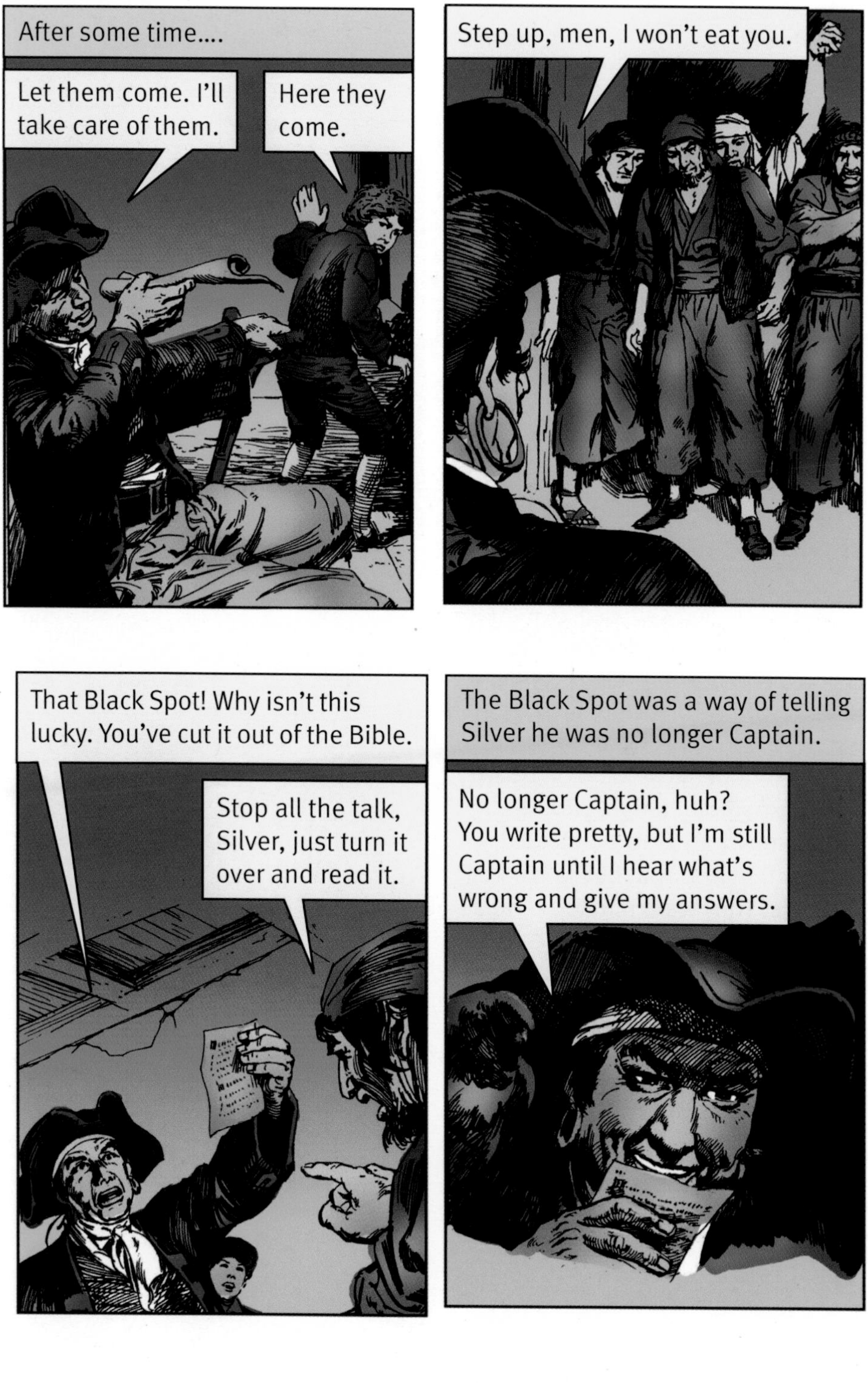
After some time....
Let them come. I'll take care of them.
Here they come.
Step up, men, I won't eat you.
That Black Spot! Why isn't this lucky. You've cut it out of the Bible.
Stop all the talk, Silver, just turn it over and read it.
The Black Spot was a way of telling Silver he was no longer Captain.
No longer Captain, huh? You write pretty, but I'm still Captain until I hear what's wrong and give my answers.

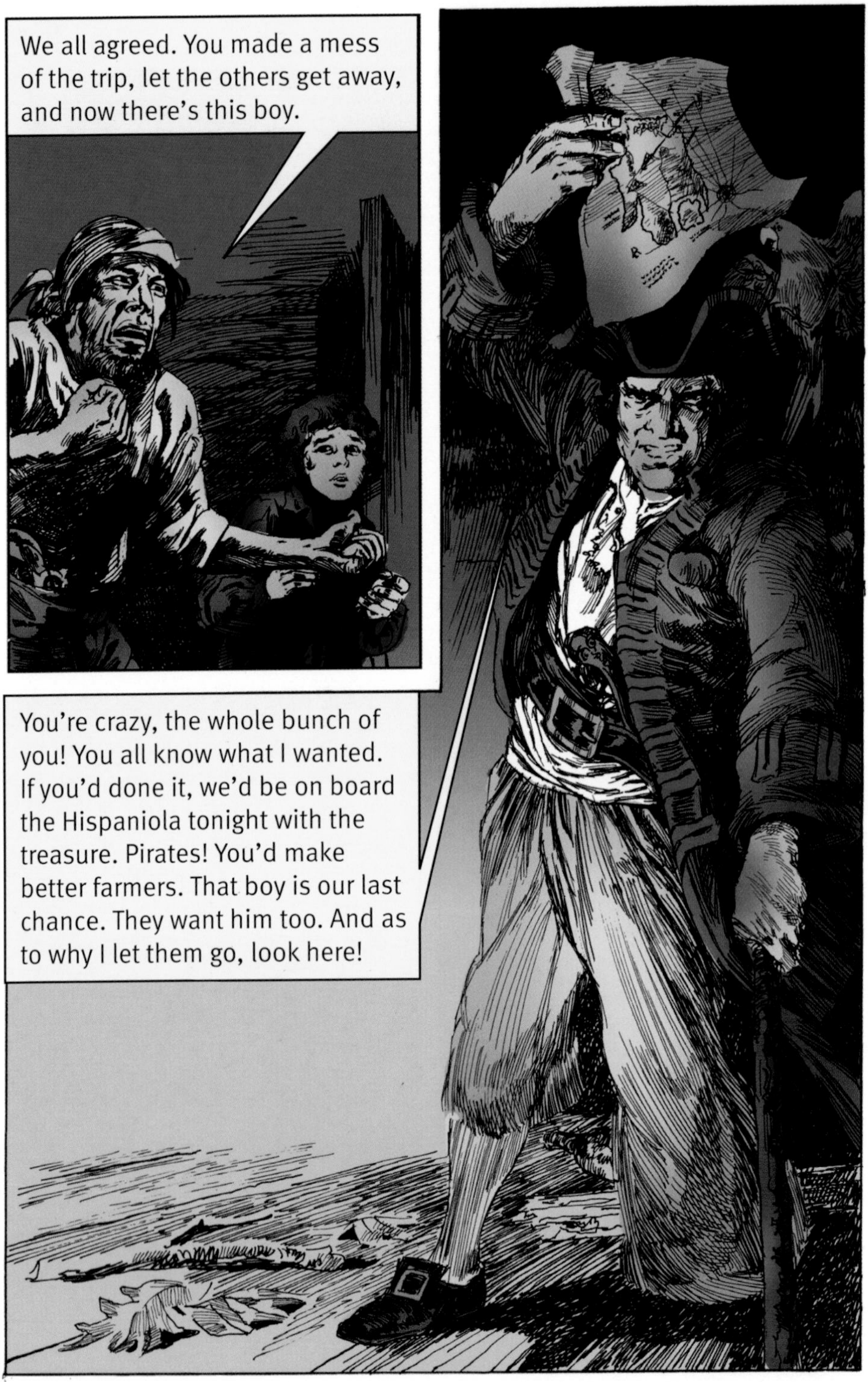
We all agreed. You made a mess of the trip, let the others get away, and now there's this boy.
You're crazy, the whole bunch of you! You all know what I wanted. If you'd done it, we'd be on board the Hispaniola tonight with the treasure. Pirates! You'd make better farmers. That boy is our last chance. They want him too. And as to why I let them go, look here!

You lost the ship, I found the treasure. Pick another Captain if you want. I'm finished talking to the likes of you.

That was the end of that.

Silver forever!

Hooray for Captain Silver!

We were awakened in the morning by a loud voice.

Silver. It's Dr. Livesey.

We're all well, Doctor, and we have a new member.

Not Jim?

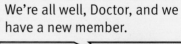

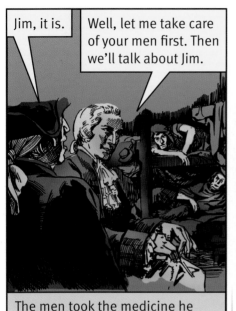

Jim, it is.

Well, let me take care of your men first. Then we'll talk about Jim.

The men took the medicine he gave them more like babies than like pirates.

Well, that takes care of everyone. Now I'd like to talk about the boy.

No!

Silver took over.

Si-lence! Doctor, I want to thank you for what you've done. I will let you speak to the boy if he promises not to run away.

I promised so....

Then, Doctor, if you'll step outside. I'll bring the boy out, and he can tell you his story.

Silver kept the men in order with looks that would kill.

Go slow, son. They might come after us if we seem to be in a hurry.

The boy will tell you I saved his life. I ask you to save mine.

Why, John, you're not afraid are you?

I'm not afraid, but I don't want to hang either. You won't forget the bad or the good I've done, I know. So I'll leave you alone to talk with the boy. Remember, no one wants to hang.

Come on, Jim. Climb the fence and we'll run for it.

You wouldn't do that and neither will I. I gave my word and so I stay. But listen...

The ship! My boy, every step of the way it's you who has saved lives.

I told him what I had done with the ship.

I want this boy kept safe, do you hear? Yell if you need help. Watch out for trouble if you find the treasure. Keep Jim safe, and if we get out of here, I'll do my best to save you.

I heard the Doctor telling you to run and you saying no. That's in your favor. Stay close to me and we'll get out of here yet!

They have the ship but once we get the treasure we'll have the upper hand.

As he talked he built up their hopes and his own as well, I'm sure.

As for the boy, why, once we've got the treasure we'll give Mr. Hawkins his share for all his help.

Silver was careful to let me know he'd try to keep me safe and keep himself from hanging.

And so we went to look for the treasure.

Following the maps, we headed
for the area between Spyglass
and Mizzenmast Hill.

Hey,
yo-ho!

This is a good piece of canvas.

There's something
strange about the way
these bones are lying.

Just looking told us the bones had been placed in a special way.

This is Flint's joke for sure. He killed all six of his men when he buried his treasure. Six men...there are six of us too.

The body lay exactly on the spot of the map we were looking for.

If ever a spirit would walk after death, it would be Flint's. He died bad.

He'd always sing "Fifteen Men" when he was getting drunk.

Stop that talking! Let's move in for the gold.

The men kept close together, frightened by the talk of spirits. All of a sudden a voice came through the trees.

They were his last words.

The men seemed less afraid now.

By God! It seemed like Ben Gunn.

It was like Flint's voice but like somebody else's too. It was like....

But Ben Gunn is just as dead as Flint.

True, but nobody minds Ben Gunn dead or alive.

And so we went on until...

We found the hiding place and saw that the treasure had been taken.

Jim, stand here.

Giving me a gun? So you're changing sides again.

Two gold coins! So you're the one who is never wrong.

Dig away, boys. You'll find more for sure.

Just then three shots rang out in the woods above us.

It seemed that Ben Gunn had found the treasure years before and hid it in his cave. When Dr. Livesey had discovered this he traded the map for the chance of getting to Ben's cave where he could be safe, have plenty of food, and help to guard the treasure.

We figured you'd be in trouble so we sent Ben out to scare you and give us time to get here and help.

If I didn't have Jim, you'd have let them cut me to pieces.

That's right, John.

We destroyed one of the boats and set out in the other to catch the Hispaniola.

Lucky for us she's still here.

Everything was fine on board.

Take us to shore and then come back and stand guard until morning.

We went to Ben's cave.

John Silver, I told you I would help you and I will, but all those men died because of you. But a promise is a promise.

Thank you for your help, sir.

You're a good boy, Jim. But I don't think we'll sail together again. You had many narrow escapes for me.

What terrible trouble had come with his treasure.

We went to work in the morning and it took us three days to get the treasure on board.

The ship loaded, we held a meeting and decided, to the great joy of Ben Gunn, to leave the three mutineers on the island with food and supplies. Then we set sail for the nearest port to hire new men for the long trip home.

We went ashore as soon as we arrived.

It's good to see so many smiling faces again.

But when we returned to the ship...

Silver's gone with a bag of our gold.

We were glad to be rid of him at last.

To make our long story short, we had a good trip home and each of us got our share of the treasure to use as we liked. We never heard of John Silver again but I'm sure he's living happily somewhere. He'd better live happily in this world for he has a poor chance at such a life in the next world.

The End